For Ameli
x x X

First published 2007 by Macmillan Children's Books
This edition published 2008 by Macmillan Children's Books
a division of Macmillan Publishers Limited
20 New Wharf Road, London N1 9RR
Basingstoke and Oxford
Associated companies throughout the world
www.panmacmillan.com

ISBN: 978-0-230-01583-8

1 3 5 7 9 8 6 4 2

A CIP catalogue record for this book is available from the British Library.

Printed in China

Emily Gravett

Macmillan Children's Books

Monkey and me,
Monkey and me,
Monkey and me,
We went to see,

We went to see some . . .

PENGUINS!

Monkey and me,

Monkey and me,

Monkey and me,

We went to see,

We went to see some . . .

KANGA

ROOS!

Monkey and me,
Monkey and me,
Monkey and me,
We went to see,

We went to see some . . .

BATS!

Monkey and me,
Monkey and me,
Monkey and me,
We went to see,

We went to see some . . .

ELEPHANTS!

Monkey and me,

Monkey and me,

Monkey and me,

We went to see,

We went to see some . . .

MON

KEYS!

Monkey . . . and . . . me,

Monkey . . . and . . . me,

Monkey . . . and . . . me,

We went . . .

. . . home for tea.

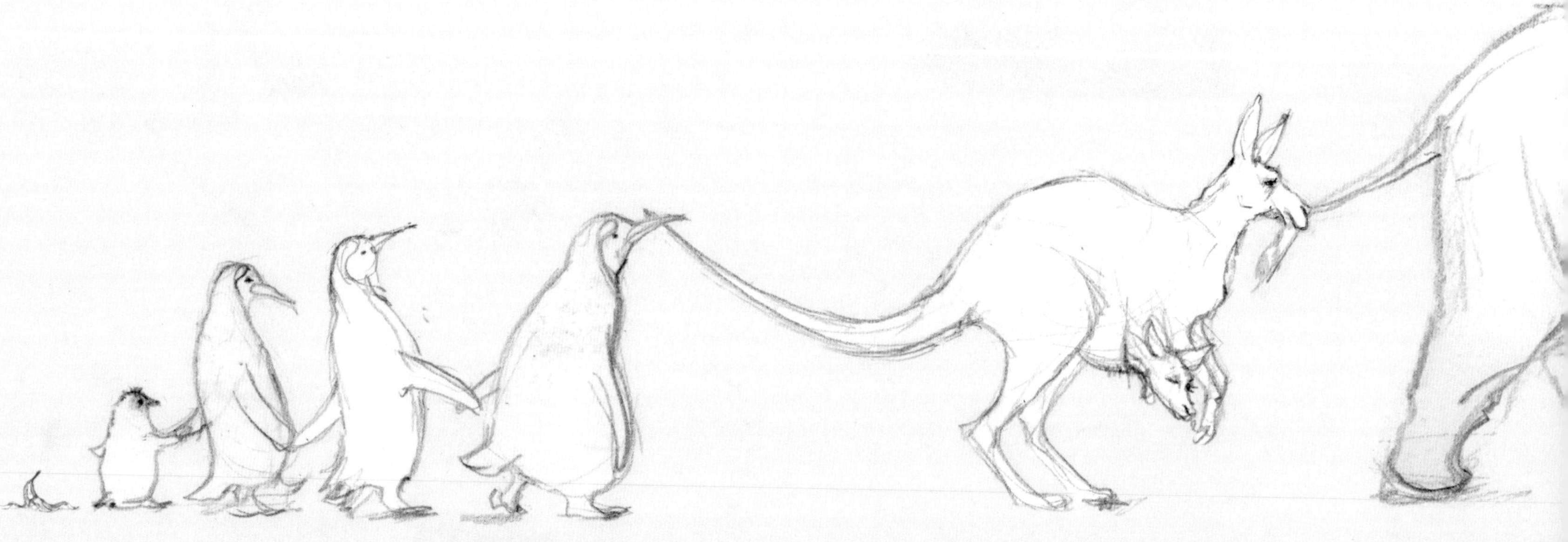

Monkey and Me
would like to say

Thank You

for reading our book.